DISNEY'S

Created by
Jim Jinkins

CHRONICLES

# Porkchop to
the Rescue

## Jim Rubin

JUMBO
PICTURES
INC.

GRADE A QUALITY

DISNEY
PRESS

New York

Illustrated by Matthew C. Peters, Tim Chi Ly and Tony Curanaj

First Edition
1 3 5 7 9 10 8 6 4 2

The artwork for this book is prepared using watercolor.
The text for this book is set 18-point New Century Schoolbook.

Library of Congress Catalog Card Number: 97-80215

ISBN: 0-7868-4231-8

Created by
Jim Jinkins

# Porkchop to the Rescue

# CHAPTER ONE

Doug and Porkchop were packing their Bluffscout gear. They were going to Yakestonia for their first ever Alpine camping trip! They would be camping with Fentruck's uncle Bazookie's scouting troop—the Yakscouts.

"You won't be camping in the Yakestonian woods by any chance, would you, Dougie?"

Doug's sister, Judy, was reading a book about exotic monsters from around the world. "That means you'll be camping near the home of the fire-breathing wart-goblin—the terror of Yakestonia!" she said.

"Judy, please don't scare your brother," said Theda.

"Scare? Who's trying to scare?" She put her arms around Doug. "I'm just trying to protect our little tendertoe from being eaten up."

Doug squirmed away. "I don't care what your book says. There aren't any

fire-breathing wart-thingies anywhere, including Yakestonia."

"Well, whatever you say, Dougie, but I'd watch my back," said Judy as she marched up to her room.

# CHAPTER TWO

The Bluffscouts and Mr. Dink clambered into the YakAir twelve-seater prop-plane. Porkchop leaped into the seat next to Doug and strapped himself in.

Roger pointed at Porkchop. Porkchop growled.

"Is that dog of yours prepared for the rigors of Alpine camping? We're going to the Yakestonian Alps, not a froofy dog show," he said.

"Porkchop's a great scout, Roger. He won't have any problems. Don't you worry," said Doug.

Roger just rolled his eyes and sat down next to Boomer.

Uncle Bazookie shook his head and giggled. "Scouting is not a normal activity for a person of the dog variety," he said to Doug. He giggled again and went into the cockpit to fire up the engines. Within minutes they were off on their adventure.

Bluffington spread out below

them like a huge map.

Doug thought he could see Patti Mayonnaise riding her bike. He drifted off to sleep with visions of Patti dancing in his head.

Many hours later, Skeeter shook Doug awake. Doug looked out the window. Tall mountains were everywhere.

"Wow."

"That's Mt. Ludnibubba," said Fentruck. "She has a fierce temper—very unpredictable weather, lots of wind. And down there is my village."

Doug looked down and saw a town that looked like Bluffington except all the houses had funny looking onion-shaped roofs.

The plane swooped down and made a screeching three-point landing on a tiny landing strip.

They were *in* Yakestonia! The Yakscouts greeted them in their tall hats, baggy short pants, and wooden clogs—the traditional Yakscout uniform.

"Man, those uniforms sure are different." Skeeter whispered to Doug.

Al Sleech nudged Moo. "These persons are not like us."

"Yes, my brother, perhaps we have landed on an alien planet," agreed Moo.

Roger took a closer look at the Yakestonian kids and realized that he was stuck with a pack of dorks.

Doug met a Yakestonian

tendertoe named Doog. He *really* looked different and strange. Roger muttered, "Whatta total worldwide loser."

Doug whispered to Skeeter, "Roger is right, these guys *are* really strange-looking."

Skeeter took a look at Doog and then looked at Doug. They could have passed for twins. "I dunno, Doug."

"Okay, Bluffscouts, gather

round," said Mr. Dink.

"Yes, it's time for the traditional Yakestonian greeting!" announced Scoutmaster Bazookie.

First, each of the Yakscouts put a hand in his armpit and squished it to make funny

sounds, then they stamped their right feet and yelled at the top of their lungs, "Zwooba, Zwooba, Zwooba!"

The Bluffscouts' jaws dropped.

Moo stammered, "By Hecuba, what have we just witnessed?"

Doug giggled. This was just *too* weird.

"I think it's some kind of hello," said Skeeter. He told everyone to give the Yakscouts the tried and true Bluffscout greeting-

*"Hecka Pecka Washa Rag,*
*Skina Dally Do,*
*Yak Scouts Yak Scouts,*
*Howdy Doody Do!"*

Now, the Yakscouts stared at
the Bluffscouts. The Yakscout,
Doog, giggled.

# CHAPTER THREE

The Yakscouts and Bluffscouts
climbed high into the hills and
finally stopped in a clearing. It
was time for dinner, or Gagstoop,
as they call it in Yakestonia. Doug,

Skeeter, and Porkchop couldn't
wait. They were really hungry!
  The Yakscouts and Scoutmaster
Bazookie sliced vegetables and

other strange stuff into a big black pot: treblinski, cornhogski, bibshorts, and spicy googlehocks.

"I don't know if I can eat this," Doug whispered to Skeeter. Skeeter looked unsure, himself.

"Traditional Yakestonian goulash!" announced Scoutmaster Bazookie.

It turned into thick soupy slop. When it was ready, Scoutmaster Bazookie ladled it into bowls.

Doog and Skeeterski pointed and giggled at their fellow Bluffscouts who were looking uneasily at the goulash.

Porkchop was not paying any attention to the scouts. He chowed down on his goulash and he liked it! Finally, Doug and Skeeter tried some, and *they* liked it, too.

"If Porkchop hadn't dared to try this, we would have starved tonight," Doug said to Skeeter.

"It is tasty," said Skeeter.
"Thanks, Porkchop!"

They went for seconds. Doug
looked up and saw Doog and
Skeeterski giggling *again*.

# CHAPTER FOUR

They finished gagstooping and Scoutmaster Bazookie said it was time for another great Yakestonian tradition.

Roger groaned. "Joeycookamonga! Another Yakscout tradition—how many can they have?"

"I dunno . . . apparently a lot," said Doug.

"This tradition is called Blab Yacky, or in your words, story-telling."

Scoutmaster Bazookie began his story: "It all started last winter when my brother, Gorgonzola, who lives downstream, saw strange animal tracks in the snow."

"What did they look like?" asked Al.

"Scary . . . Very unusual."

"Big?" asked Skeeter, in a quavering voice.

"Yes, very big."

"Wartgoblin size?" asked Doug.

Soutmaster Bazookie just continued his story.

"Every morning when he woke up, things had been moved around in the house as if someone or something had been there. One morning he noticed his sausages were missing. Then his pot of goulash disappeared.

"That's when Gorgonzola realized that the footprints were the footprints of a fire-breathing wartgoblin."

All the scouts gasped.

"One morning, he went down-stairs to the kitchen, expecting the usual wartgoblin mischief. But nothing seemed to be missing. Then he saw a crumpled piece of paper on the kitchen table.

"It said 'HUNGRY REALLY HUNGRY.' My brother gulped.

"That night he laid out the last of his food. He hoped that would satisfy the wartgoblin. The next morning, the food was gone. But there was another note: 'STILL HUNGRY.' My brother was terri-fied—there was no more food . . . except for him. What was the wartgoblin going to do? Was he,

Gorgonzola, next on the wartgoblin's menu? He shook in his boots. He decided to come to me for help.

"Luckily my brother escaped the wartgoblin and arrived on my doorstep tired and cold, but still in one piece."

"And that's the end of the story?" asked Skeeter.

"No . . . not at all. I thought you should all know. I found this note at this campsite when we arrived." He lifted it up in the air for everyone to see. It said in big red letters: STILL HUNGRY!!

Someone yelled, "Wartgoblin!"

Suddenly, a howling wind

ripped through the campsite,
blowing something over Doug's
head. Everything went black.

Doug ran for all he was worth—
away from the campsite. Then he

tripped over a rotten tree stump
and hit his head. When he
reached up to rub it, he realized
what had happened.

He pulled a tent off his head. A
wartgoblin had not blown the
campfire out and attacked him. A

huge gust of wind had knocked a tent over and it had landed on him. Now he was in the middle of a strange forest where wartgoblins might really be lurking.

He called out, "Yoo hoo, guys, anyone out there? Skeeter? Porkchop?" But no one answered.

# CHAPTER FIVE

Doug heard footsteps and he thought, Great . . . here I am in the middle of nowhere. Why didn't I listen to Judy? I should have *never* come on this trip! I'll be slapped on a giant piece of

wartgoblin rye toast and never
see home or Patti again!

He ran through the Yakestonian
woods. Then he tripped and slid
down a muddy ravine. The footsteps
were still behind him. He turned
around and—THUMP—he ran
straight into . . . he wasn't sure what.

He gulped. But when Doug
looked closely he saw it was just a

kid wrapped up in a tent. Exactly what had happened to him!

Doug helped the kid get untangled, and it was Doog, the Yakscout he had thought was really strange and different.

"Doog!"

"Doug!"

"I'm sure glad it was you and not some scout-eating wartgoblin," said Doug.

"Me as well," said Doog.

As they eyed each other for a second, Doug realized that *this* was the kid who had been giggling at him. But he was glad that he had run into him and not a fire-breathing wartgoblin.

# CHAPTER SIX

Tents and camping gear were scattered all over the woods around the campsite. Pots and pans hung from trees and the tents were flattened.

"The angry winds of Mt. Ludnibubba have hit!" exclaimed Fentruck.

Skeeterski, the Yakscout who was Doog's friend, looked worried. He came over to Skeeter and said, "I worry for my friend. OOGA OOGA."

"I worry for *my* friend, too. HONK HONK!" Skeeter answered.

"Not to worry! Not to worry!" Mr. Dink appeared with a funny-looking hat. Wires, pulleys, and hoses noodled in and out of it.

"Boys, you may be saying to yourself, 'What is that thing?' Well, let me say that it will find Doug and Doog in a jiffy. This is an official Yakestonian Alpine survival hat." He pushed a button on the side. A big nose-shaped thing popped out with two flood-lights next to it. He added, "It's got twice the scent-sniffing power of a normal dog. Very expensive."

Porkchop frowned.

"Not so sure, Porkchop?" asked Skeeter. Porkchop just shook his head. No way would Mr. Dink find Doug and Doog with that!

"Whatta *you* think, guys?"
Skeeter asked Al and Moo Sleech.

"Oh, wise one, that artificial
olfactory protuberance does not
look like it is of sound design,"
said Al.

"Negative twenty-one to the third power," added Moo in agreement.

Mr. Dink was not paying attention to the scouts. "Be back in a second, boys," he said as he tromped off into the woods with the contraption teetering on his head.

# CHAPTER SEVEN

"What should we do?" asked Doog.

"Well," said Doug, "I was thinking we could climb one of these tall trees. We might see the campsite."

Doog giggled. "No, my friend, Billibob trees are poisonous to touch this time of year."

"Why are you always giggling at me?" Doug blurted out.

"Why do you giggle at me?" Doog shouted back.

Doug stopped and thought for a second. He *had* laughed at him.

"Well-l-l . . ." Doug didn't really know what to say.

Doog cut in. "I am sorry, Doug, but I laughed because I think you are nebinski and trollski."

"Oh," Doug said. "I was laughing at *you* 'cause I thought you were really different and strange and by the way, what does nebinski and trollski mean?"

"I think it means different and strange," Doog said.

"Oh, trollski, nebinski!" Doug laughed. "We are *both* nebinski and trollski."

They laughed.

"Well, now what should we do?" asked Doug.

"Do you hear that?" asked Doog.

"It's a

stream," Doug answered.

"Yes, and it must lead back to
the campsite," said Doog.

Yakscout and Bluffscout hopped
from rock to rock in the stream,
until they saw a flickering light.

"Doug, observe. It is the campfire. We are almost there."

"Woohoo!" Doug cheered until he noticed that the light bobbed up and down . . . kind of like a fire-breathing wartgoblin!

# CHAPTER 8

"It's moving," Doug whispered.
They both stood still.

A towering dark figure with
horns rushed by, waving its
menacing claws. "Ahhhhhh!!" it

yelled. It looked like fire was coming out of its mouth.

As suddenly as it appeared, it was gone.

Doug, teeth chattering and legs shaking from fear, looked around. Doog was gone, too. He had run away screaming. When Doug found him, the two scouts dragged themselves back upstream. Their campsite was deserted.

"Hello?!" Doug cried out. "Where is everybody, Doog?"

Porkchop ran out of the woods and jumped into Doug's arms.

"Whoa, Porkchop, where'd everyone go? What happened?"

43

asked
Doug.
Porkchop
barked
and
pointed
frantically
toward
the woods.
Doug
moved to
follow him.
"Doug,
nice warm
fire *here*;
crazed
monster running around in dark
creepy woods *there*. Do you think

it's good idea to go there?" asked Doog.

Doug replied, "If Porkchop thinks this is the right thing to do, it's the right thing to do."

# CHAPTER NINE

The darkness closed around
them as they followed Porkchop.
Soon they heard whooping and
hollering.

"Hey, look, there they are!" cried
Doug.

They found all the boys and Yakscout leader Bazookie in a big circle, yelling and waving their arms. They were closing in on something.

Uncle Bazookie turned to Doug. His brow was covered with sweat.

"Doug, Doog, thank goodness you are unharmed. We feared you had been seized by . . ." He pointed at the center of the circle. "The wartgoblin! It panics me that Scoutmaster Dink may be in his clutches."

The monster looked stunned and confused as it waved its arms around. It had sticklike horns and slimy-looking skin. It slobbered and sputtered and sounded a little like . . . Mr. Dink?

The strange creature turned toward Roger. Roger panicked and begged for his life, "Please don't eat me! Eat *them*! Eat *them*!"

"Careful, scouts. Don't hurt it. It must be captured alive!" said Scoutmaster Bazookie.

The situation was getting out of hand. Someone had to do something. So Porkchop raced through everyone's legs and bravely jumped up into the monster's arms.

GASP!! Fear gripped Doug's heart. Would Porkchop be the wartgoblin's next snack?

But Porkchop was calm. He reached up and rubbed the monster's face. Sticks, mud, and moss came off in his paw.

It *was* Mr. Dink!

Roger brushed himself off. "I knew it was Dink all along," he told the others.

"Oh, thank you, Porkchop," Mr. Dink gasped. "It was dark and scary in there!"

"Everything okay, Mr. Dink?" asked Doug.

"Oh, hello, Douglas. This sniffer-outer machine really *does* work. Found you guys in a jiffy. What'd I tell you?" Mr. Dink did not know what had happened.

"Mr. Dink, they thought you were a monster! Lucky Porkchop wasn't afraid."

Scoutmaster Bazookie lifted up

Porkchop. "Without this extraordinary animal, Bud Dink might have become exhibition for zoo. I am so sorry I questioned your presence for this expedition. You are hero, Porkchop."

All the scouts cheered for Porkchop, "Hip, hip, hooray!"

"So who wrote that 'STILL

HUNGRY' note that you found at the campsite?" asked Mr. Dink after the cheering had calmed down. "That scared the dickens out of me."

"I confess," said Bazookie. "I wrote the note. Yakestonian tradition: always cap off campfire story with note written by the scary monster."

# CHAPTER TEN

Doug couldn't wait to get off the plane because he had so many things he wanted to show his family.

When he saw his family, he stuck his hand in his armpit, stomped his foot, and yelled,

"Zwooba, zwooba, zwooba! It's a Yakestonian tradition!"

His family just stared.

"Dougie," said Judy. "It's a first, but I'm speechless."

"Porkchop and I have even more Yakestonian traditions to show you."

"How many traditions do they have?" his mother asked.

"A lot," said Doug, "and they're *all* nebinski and trollski!"

# A BRAND SPANKING NEW BOOK SERIES

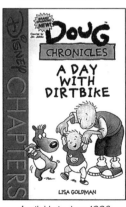